THE PUPPY

SSF

FLASH

Meet all the puppies at The Puppy Place!

Goldie

Snowball

Shadow

Rascal

Buddy

THE PUPPY PLACE

FLASH

ELLEN
MILES

A
LITTLE APPLE
PAPERBACK

SCHOLASTIC INC.

New York   London   Toronto   Auckland   Sydney
Mexico City   Hong Kong   New Delhi   Buenos Aires

For Bec, Larry, and Bodi
—E.M.

ISBN-13: 978-0-439-87411-3
ISBN-10: 0-439-87411-4

12 11 10 9 8 7 6   7 8 9 10 11/0

Printed in the U.S.A.   40

First printing, November 2006

THE PUPPY PLACE

FLASH

CHAPTER ONE

"Ohhh, I'm so full!" Charles patted his belly. "I can't eat any more."

"Really?" Aunt Abigail asked. "So, you won't be having any chocolate cream pie?"

"Well . . ." Charles said, "maybe just a tiny piece." He looked down at the little tan puppy lying near his feet. Charles did want dessert, but he also really wanted to play with Buddy, who had been waiting so patiently through Thanksgiving dinner.

"Uh-huh," said Mom. "And a piece of apple pie, too, probably, and some berry crumble."

"Yup," said Charles. "I still have my dessert stomach!" That was what the Petersons called it when you were too full for real food but still had

1

room for dessert. Charles never said no to dessert, no matter how full he was. And Aunt Abigail's desserts were the best. She was once the pastry chef for a fancy hotel in New York City, so she really knew what she was doing.

Now she and Uncle Stephen lived out in the country. Six months ago, they had given up their busy city lives to move to this old farm at the end of a long country road. Now they had busy *country* lives. Aunt Abigail was working in the old-fashioned farmhouse kitchen baking cakes and pies that she sold at the town's general store, and Uncle Stephen worked on a computer upstairs doing the same business stuff (Charles wasn't sure exactly what it was) he had done in the city. "Only with a better view," Uncle Stephen always said.

The Petersons had visited the farm before, but this was their first Thanksgiving there. Mom and Dad and Lizzie, Charles's older sister, and the Bean, his younger brother, had all piled into their van (Dad's red pickup didn't have enough room for all of them) along with Buddy, their puppy. They had driven for what felt like a whole day, stopping every hour to let Buddy out for a little play-and-pee time.

The drive was boring — how many hours can you stand to play license-plate bingo? — but Charles thought it was worth it to see his cousins. Or at least it was worth it to see Becky, the one who was the same age as Charles. They were both in second grade. Becky was cool. And really brave. She would climb the highest tree in the yard, swim in the coldest stream, ride her bike down the steepest hill. Becky loved mysteries and playing detective. She loved her new home in the country.

On the other hand, Stephanie, her older sister, was kind of a pain. She was in fifth grade, and she thought she knew everything. (Just like Lizzie, Charles thought. Maybe older sisters were all alike.) And she hated living on the farm. Steph never stopped talking about how boring the country was and how much she missed high-speed Internet, fun stores, and good Chinese restaurants.

If anything was boring, thought Charles, it was having to hear about how great New York City was. How Macy's was the biggest department store and the Knicks were the best basketball team, blah, blah, blah.

Lizzie didn't seem to mind Stephanie. Charles thought that was probably because she and Stephanie were like two bossy, know-it-all peas in a pod. Plus, they both loved horses, and they could go on and on forever about riding and saddles and grooming.

On the drive over, Mom had said to be nice to Stephanie because she was "having a hard time with the move." And it was true that Steph had been more fun back when the Petersons would visit their cousins in New York. She had even helped them get autographs from some of the Yankees when they all went to a baseball game together.

Still, Charles would rather hang out with Becky. They had been having a blast playing with Buddy. Becky could not get over how lucky Charles was to have his own puppy.

Charles couldn't get over it, either. Sometimes it was still hard for him to believe that Buddy was theirs for keeps. The Petersons had fostered lots of puppies, giving them a safe home until they found the perfect "forever home" for each one. But no matter how much Lizzie, Charles, and the Bean had begged, they had never been allowed to keep a puppy themselves. Until Buddy came along, that is.

The Petersons had taken care of Buddy and his two sisters when they were all just tiny puppies, and everyone in the family had fallen in love with him. Buddy was the runt of the litter, smaller and more timid than his sisters, and he needed extra care.

Buddy was mostly tan, with chocolate-brown markings and a white heart on his chest. He was the sweetest, smartest, funniest puppy ever. Charles never got tired of playing with him, holding him, and even just watching while Buddy did regular puppy things like eating his breakfast or chewing on a puppy toy.

As soon as dinner was over, Charles and Becky asked to be excused. "We'll take Buddy for a walk," offered Charles. The puppy jumped up as soon as he heard that word. He wagged his tail so hard that his whole body wriggled. "Hold on, hold on!" Charles laughed as Buddy licked his face while he tried to clip on the squirmy pup's leash. Outside, Buddy pulled Charles this way and that as he ran to sniff all the new, exciting smells. It was already almost dark, and the air was cold and clear.

"Let's pretend Buddy is a pirate and he's leading us to where his treasure is buried," said Becky.

"Because we captured his ship," Charles added, getting into the game. "And now he has to show us the hiding place, or we'll make him walk the plank."

Buddy made a pretty silly pirate. He kept sniffing every bush and fence post he came across. His leash was getting all tangled as he darted here and there through the yard. "Wait up!" said Charles as Buddy circled back toward the house.

"Look! It's another pirate ship!" Becky said, pointing to a car that was coming up the long dirt road that led to the farm. Its headlights lit up the house as it drew closer. It pulled right up to where Charles and Becky were standing, near the front door.

The car stopped, and a lady got out. She was holding a bundle in her arms, a bundle that wriggled and moved. It was something wrapped in a blanket. Charles couldn't figure out what it might be.

The lady started talking — *fast*. "Sorry to drop Flash off in such a hurry, but we're in a terrible rush," she said, her words tumbling over one another. "Murray's father took sick, so we're leaving much sooner than we thought. We'll be driving all night long as it is! Of course he's had all his shots and everything, as you can tell by his tags — oops! I forgot his collar. Oh, well. Anyway, I'm sure he'll be a big help to you, and we sure do appreciate that he has a good place to stay and all, and —"

"Dot! Let's go already!" said a man's voice from inside the car.

"Okay, okay!" The woman gave the bundle in her arms a big kiss. "We'll miss you, Flash," she said. Then she gently put it down on the ground and hopped back into the car. "He's a little shy! Just give him time and you'll see how sweet he is," was the last thing the woman called out as the car turned around in the driveway. A moment later, the car was on its way back down the driveway, leaving Charles and Becky staring at each other — and at the bundle. Buddy strained at his leash, trying to get a sniff of whatever it was.

"What was *that* all about?" Charles asked.

"I have no idea," said Becky. She stepped forward and unfolded the blanket.

"Oh!" said Charles.

There, looking up at him, was the cutest black-and-white puppy he had ever seen.

CHAPTER TWO

Flash wasn't a small, roly-poly puppy like Buddy. He was a sleek, long-legged, pointy-nosed dog. But Charles could tell by the way he sprang to his feet when Becky unwrapped the blanket that he wasn't a grown-up dog. He was black and white, with a silky coat and a long, feathered tail. His black eyes were shiny and bright. This puppy had obviously been loved and well cared for.

"Oh, my gosh!" said Becky. "He's so cute!" She reached out a hand to pet him.

Charles saw the puppy's tail droop down as he crouched, ready to run. "Hold on," he said to Becky, putting a hand on her arm. "That lady was right. He *is* shy."

Flash sniffed, and listened, and looked, learning as much as he could about these people. It was important to know as much as you could. And always be ready to run.

Becky slowed down. "So, what do we do?" she asked.

"Just inch forward slowly," Charles said. "So we don't scare him." He reached down to pick Buddy up, so his little tan puppy wouldn't bound forward and scare the black-and-white puppy off.

Hey! Hold on! I was just about to go meet my new friend! Buddy licked Charles's face. Sometimes when he did that, Charles laughed and put him down. Not this time.

Charles and Becky took one baby step at a time, trying to get closer to the puppy without scaring him away. He crouched down, watching them intently. His long tail was waving slowly back and forth.

"Buddy!" Charles cried as the squirming puppy in his arms struggled and kicked and pushed himself out of Charles's grip. Charles grabbed Buddy's leash. But it was too late. Buddy galloped toward the other puppy. The white-and-black pup dashed back toward the fence near the driveway with his tail between his legs. He stood behind a fence post, eyeing them warily.

"Now what?" Becky asked. "Should we go get the grown-ups? Or Steph and Lizzie?"

"No way," Charles said. "If Lizzie gets involved, she'll just get all bossy."

Becky nodded. "Steph is the same way. And they're worse when they're together. They'll just gang up on us and take over."

Lizzie thought she knew everything about dogs. But Charles knew a few things, too. "I think we can handle this ourselves."

"Okay, so what do we do?" Becky was ready for action.

Charles thought for a second. "Let's try this," he suggested. "We'll walk away, toward the barn, like we forgot all about him and have something more interesting to do. That sometimes works with Buddy when we're out in the yard and he won't come when I call. If he gets curious enough, he'll come running after me when I go the other way."

"Okay," said Becky, shrugging. "So, we pretend like we don't care? It's worth a try."

She and Charles turned their backs to Flash and started walking toward the barn. Buddy led the way, with his tail up and his chest out.

Buddy wasn't sure where they were going, or why, but he wanted to be part of it. He'd be in front!

Charles peeked back over his shoulder. "It's working!" he whispered to Becky. "He's following us!"

Sure enough, the black-and-white pup was trotting along right behind them with a quizzical look in his alert, shiny eyes.

Good! A job! Just what Flash needed, when he was so unsure about this new place. These people needed to be herded along. He would make sure they stayed together and kept moving.

The dog followed them right into the musty, dark barn. "Great," Charles said in a low tone. "We've got him inside, where he's safe. I didn't want him running away. If he went down to the main road, he might get hit by a car."

"We can get him into an even safer place," Becky said. "There's an old horse stall down at the end. Dad said maybe Steph could have a horse someday." She groped around by the door. "Where's that light switch — there it is!" She switched on the lights. In their dim glow, Charles saw a rusty red tractor parked near the door.

"I hope Flash will follow us all the way there," Charles said. "Hold on. I'm going to tie Buddy up so he doesn't get in the way." He looped Buddy's leash around the steering wheel of the tractor. Buddy whined a little.

Hey! Why do I have to be tied up? I want to play with my new friend!

But when Charles told him to "stay," Buddy sat down and looked hopeful. Charles dug into his pocket and pulled out a few tiny dog treats. "Here you go." He tossed one to Buddy. "Good boy." Lizzie's training routine sure was paying off. They worked with the puppy a little bit every day, and Buddy was already much better behaved than lots of grown-up dogs.

Charles glanced back at the black-and-white puppy. "Maybe Flash likes treats, too," he said. He kept a few in his hand.

He and Becky walked toward the back of the

barn. Flash followed them closely, his head down and his tail held out straight.

"There's the stall," Becky whispered, pointing toward a chin-high wooden door.

"Go on inside," Charles told his cousin, pulling the swinging door open. He slipped into the stall behind Becky, still holding on to the door. The puppy stuck his head around the corner, peeking inside to see where they had gone. Charles and Becky stopped. Then Flash moved forward slowly, step by careful step.

As soon as the puppy was inside the stall, Charles pulled the door shut, sealing the three of them inside.

When he saw Charles move and heard the sound of the door closing, Flash sprang around and tried to escape. But there was no exit. The puppy looked back at Charles and Becky with wild eyes.

*　　*　　*

Flash had never been comfortable with strangers. Most people were nice once you got to know them, but you could never be sure. Flash wished his own people would come back and get him out of this place. He didn't like feeling trapped.

"It's okay," Charles said soothingly. "We won't hurt you. It's okay." Slowly, he held out the hand with the dog treats in it.

Flash blinked and he took one step closer.

Charles held his breath. His hand was shaking a little. The woman had said that Flash was a sweetie, but you never knew with a strange dog. It was good to be careful. The puppy took three quick steps forward, gently snatched a treat from Charles's hand, and stepped back to gulp it down.

"Good boy!" Charles said. He turned to Becky. "So, now he's safe and sound. The next question is, what is he *doing* here?"

Becky's eyes were shining. "It's a mystery!"

CHAPTER THREE

"A mystery!" Charles looked from Becky to the puppy. "Hey, you're right!"

The puppy had calmed down a little. Now he was sitting alertly in a corner of the stall, watching Charles and Becky with intelligent eyes. One ear stood up, and the other fell halfway over. He was a real cutie.

"Well, we know your name is Flash," Becky said.

"And you're a boy. Hello, Flash," Charles said softly.

Flash held up a paw.

It was good to hear his name. Maybe these children weren't exactly strangers, after all! Maybe he could trust them.

Down at the other end of the barn, Buddy had started to whine. He didn't like being separated from Charles. "It's okay, pal," Charles called. "I'll be there soon." He turned to Becky. "What should we do?" he asked.

Becky thought for a minute. "Let's not tell anyone else yet. Let's keep him in here and see if we can solve the mystery of who those people were and why they brought him here."

Charles liked that idea. It was exactly the kind of idea that Sammy, his best friend at home, would have come up with. "Cool," he said. "We'll have to bring him something to eat. We only brought enough puppy food for Buddy, so we'll have to give him people food until we can buy more dog chow." He paused. "We should get a blanket, too. But how will we get all that stuff out here without anybody noticing?"

Becky laughed. "I bet our dads are both snoozing, one on each couch. Stephanie and

Lizzie are probably in the den watching a video, and our moms are sitting by the fire, yakking."

Charles nodded. "You're probably right. And the Bean is probably asleep on my mom's lap. That's how Thanksgiving usually ends up. I bet they've hardly even noticed that we're gone."

"Just to be safe," Becky said, "how about if you go in and distract them while I find some food in the kitchen? Then we can meet up and come back out here."

"Um, okay," Charles agreed. He didn't have a clue about how he would "distract" everyone, but Becky seemed so sure of herself that he figured it must be a good plan. Maybe he could tell his latest knock-knock joke! That would be perfect. Mom and Dad had only heard it about four or five times so far, on the way to the farm.

"We'll be back soon," Charles told Flash. The dog still wasn't ready to be petted, but he seemed to understand that Charles and Becky were going to help him. He sighed softly as he curled up in the hay.

Buddy was so happy to see Charles again that he twirled around three times as Charles unhooked his leash from the tractor. He licked Charles's hands and made joyful snuffling noises. "Good boy, Buddy," Charles said. "Good boy."

When they got inside the house, Becky and Charles split up. Charles headed for the living room. Sure enough, the scene was exactly as he and Becky had pictured it. Dad was snoring softly on the blue couch, and Uncle Stephen was on the flowered one. Lizzie and Stephanie were in the den watching some goopy love movie. Buddy ran right in and jumped up on Lizzie's lap when Charles peeked in the door. Mom and Aunt Abigail were sitting by the fire, talking quietly. The only surprise was that the Bean was on Aunt Abigail's lap instead of Mom's. Nobody really seemed to need distracting, but Charles had a job to do. He got right to work.

"Hey, Mom," he said. "Knock, knock!"

His mom sighed. Sometimes Charles had a feeling that she was tired of knock-knock jokes, but how could that be? He was always coming up with new ones. It wasn't like he told the same one over and over. Not too many times, anyway.

"Who's there?" Aunt Abigail asked.

"Lena," said Charles.

"Lena who?" Aunt Abigail said gamely.

"Lena little closer and I'll tell you!" Charles waited for her to laugh.

Instead, Aunt Abigail sat up straight and looked toward the kitchen. "What's that noise?" she asked.

Charles heard a clatter. Becky must have knocked something over. Charles gulped. "Oh, that's just Becky," he said quickly. "She said she was going to get something to eat." He wasn't lying. Becky *was* getting something to eat. It just wasn't for herself — but he left that part out.

"How can she be *hungry*?" Mom said, rubbing her belly with a little groan. "I'm still stuffed."

Charles shrugged. "Well, anyway, maybe I'll go find her," he said. By now, he just wanted to get out of the room. This job of distracting people made him nervous. Besides, he wanted to get back to the barn to make sure Flash was okay. "Oh, by the way," he added casually, looking at Aunt Abigail, "do you know somebody named Murray?"

"Murray?" Aunt Abigail rubbed her chin, thinking. "Do you mean the bald guy who delivers bread to the store?"

"Maybe," Charles said. He hadn't gotten a good look at the man in the car. Maybe he was bald. "Does he live around here?"

"I have no idea," Aunt Abigail said. "Mrs. Daniels down at the store might know." She gave Charles a curious look. "Why do you ask?"

"Uh —" Charles wasn't sure what to say. Luckily,

just then there was another crash from the kitchen. "No reason, really," Charles said, backing out of the room. "I'll just go help Becky. See ya!"

That was close.

"Eesh!" Charles said, when he came into the kitchen. "Don't ask me to do *that* again." Becky's arms were loaded up with a blanket, a metal bowl, a gallon jug of water, and a plastic container full of leftover turkey.

"We're all set, I think," she said. "Are they suspicious?"

"Not very," Charles said, looking over his shoulder. "But let's get out of here, anyway. Flash is probably hungry."

He *was* hungry. The puppy gobbled down three big pieces of turkey in about three seconds. Then he looked eagerly up at Charles and Becky, as if to ask for more.

At least they had good food at this place. And this little room was cozy enough. Flash didn't like being locked in, but he would find a way out as soon as he had a chance. Maybe then he could get back to his own people. Meanwhile, as long as these children kept bringing him food, he might as well hang around.

By the time Flash had finished all the turkey, he seemed to consider Charles and Becky his friends. He nudged their hands with his nose, looking for pats, and even licked Charles's cheek. They sat for a few minutes in a corner of the stall, petting the silky puppy and talking about how to solve the mystery. Then it was time to head inside, before the grown-ups realized they were missing.

CHAPTER FOUR

Becky set her alarm clock for six in the morning so they could get up to feed and walk Flash before anybody else was out of bed. She tiptoed into the den, where Charles was sleeping on the pullout couch, and shook him awake. Luckily, Buddy had decided to sleep in Stephanie's room with Stephanie and Lizzie, so he didn't beg to come outside with them.

It was still dark when they stepped out the back door. Cold, too. Charles's breath came out in little white puffs, and he pulled his hands up inside his jacket sleeves to keep them warm.

Becky had a flashlight with her, and they used it to light their way into the barn and down the aisle to the stall where Flash was waiting.

"Hey, Flash," Charles called softly. "Good morning! It's us!"

Flash woke up in a hurry. He was glad to see the boy and girl. They had been nice to him, and they had brought him delicious food. Maybe they had something good this time, too!

When they opened the stall door, Flash jumped right up and trotted over to sniff Becky's hand and let her pet him. "He likes us now," Becky said.

"He trusts us," Charles said. "He knows we'll take care of him, don't you, boy?" He gave Flash's head a little rub.

"I bet he'll like *this*," Becky said, opening the lid of the container she'd brought out to the barn. "Some leftover stuffing and mashed potatoes with gravy."

Flash wolfed down the food and looked eagerly for more.

"We'd better buy him some real puppy food,"

Charles said. "Somebody's going to notice if we keep taking food from the fridge. Plus, he's a dog. Dog food is better for him than people food." Charles didn't really know why that was. Buddy's kibble sure didn't look or smell all that tasty. But Dr. Gibson, their vet, had said that it was the best thing for a growing puppy to be eating.

"Great idea," said Becky. "We were going to the store, anyway."

That was what they had decided the night before. They'd already found out that a man named Murray delivered bread to the store. It seemed like the perfect place to start their detective work. If they could find out who Murray was, and where he had gone, then maybe they could track him down. Surely he and his wife didn't *mean* to abandon Flash at a stranger's farm.

Charles had brought Buddy's leash with him. He clipped it onto Flash's collar, and he and Becky took Flash out into the cold, dark yard. The dog pulled eagerly at the leash, dashing this way and that to check out every smell. "Come on, Flash," Charles begged. "Do your business!" The sun was going to come up any minute, and they had to have Flash back in the barn before that.

Finally, Flash did what Charles wanted him to do.

"Good boy!" Charles said. They took him back into the barn and got him settled into his stall. "We'll be back soon," Charles promised, scratching Flash between the ears. Flash leaned against Charles's leg with a contented sigh. Charles hated to leave, but if he and Becky didn't show up for breakfast, their parents would start wondering.

When they slipped into the house, Charles heard voices from the bright, warm kitchen. Everybody was up, although Stephanie and Lizzie were still in their p.j.'s. Buddy was padding around the kitchen, sniffing the floor as he checked for food scraps. "I'll take Buddy out," Charles volunteered quickly. What if Flash started barking or something? For now it was better if everybody stayed inside, far from the barn.

Afterward, Charles sat down at the table and had a big piece of apple pie, just like Dad and Uncle Stephen. Pie for breakfast was a special Peterson family Thanksgiving tradition. Dessert for breakfast! Charles wished all family traditions were that cool. When he was done, he looked over at Becky. "Ready?" he mouthed.

She nodded. "Mom, we're going for a walk," Becky said. "Just to the store."

"Why bother?" Stephanie asked, making a face. "There's nothing there but fly swatters and old cans of beans."

"Steph, come on!" said Aunt Abigail. "That store is full of lovely things. Including my baked goods, if I do say so myself!"

"Yeah," said Lizzie. "I love the penny candy they sell. That store's not so bad."

"Easy for you to say," said Stephanie grumpily.

"You get to live in a place where there are normal stores and malls and everything."

"Well, we're going, anyway," Becky said.

"What's your hurry?" Lizzie gave Charles a suspicious look.

He knew it! It was nearly impossible to hide anything from Nosy Lizzie.

"No hurry." Charles shrugged. "We just feel like going for a walk."

"Bundle up!" said Mom without looking at Charles. She was busy reading the paper as she ate some leftover berry crumble.

It was only a ten-minute walk to the store, just long enough for Becky and Charles to figure out a good plan for what to do when they got there. They had a few clues to their mystery, and they needed to find out more.

Charles breathed in a deep, happy sniff when he and Becky walked in, jingling the bell on the door. The store had squeaky wooden floors, and it smelled like chocolate and fresh bread and furniture polish, which turned out to be a really good combination.

They approached the woman at the cash register. "Hi, Mrs. Daniels," said Becky. "Remember Charles?"

"Sure," said Mrs. Daniels. "Mr. Knock-knock Joke, right?"

Charles nodded. Perfect. This fit right in with the plan he and Becky had made. "Knock-knock," he said. (This was part one of the plan.)

"Who's there?" asked Mrs. Daniels, with a smile.

"Murray," said Charles.

"Murray who?"

"Murray Christmas to all, and to all a good night!" Charles couldn't help laughing at his own joke.

Mrs. Daniels chuckled, too. "That's a good one," she said.

"Speaking of Murray," Becky said, taking over

with part two of the plan. "Isn't Murray your bread delivery man?"

Charles slipped away to look over the dog food choices while Becky asked Mrs. Daniels some questions. "Murray?" Charles heard the store owner say. "You know, he hasn't been around for a couple of days. We've had a substitute driver delivering our bread. . . . No, I don't know Murray's last name, or where he lives. Sorry!"

"Well, that was a dead end," Becky said as they left the store.

"At least we got something for Flash to eat!" Charles pointed out. He was carrying a bag of puppy chow. It had cost most of two weeks' allowance. "Let's go visit him and figure out what to do next," Charles said as they turned up the long driveway that led to the farm.

He was so excited to see Flash, he didn't notice Lizzie watching from the living room window as they walked past the house.

CHAPTER FIVE

But Lizzie noticed Charles. She and Stephanie raced out to the barn and cornered Charles and Becky before they could get inside Flash's stall.

"I knew it!" Lizzie stood with her hands on her hips, shaking her head. "I just *knew* you two were up to something!"

Stephanie reached for the door of the stall. "Come on, what do you have in there?"

Charles groaned. It hadn't even been twenty-four hours! He must have been kidding himself that he could keep a secret from Lizzie, the biggest busybody in the world. She always had to be in the know about everything. And obviously, Stephanie was the same way.

Charles looked at Becky.

34

Becky looked at Charles.

"Oh, well," Charles said. "I guess you'd have found out sooner or later." He pushed open the door of the stall. "Meet Flash," he said.

"Oh!" said Stephanie. She got down on her knees. "Come here, you cutie!" She held out a gentle hand to Flash. He was used to people by now, and he walked right over to sniff Stephanie.

"Wow," said Lizzie. "This isn't exactly what I expected." She looked impressed. "How long have you two been hiding a dog in here?"

"For a while," Charles said. But, at the same time, Becky said, "Since last night." Charles made a face at Becky. He didn't want to tell their sisters any more than they had to.

But Lizzie just nodded. "What a beautiful border collie," she said. "Judging by its size, I'd say it's about six months old." Lizzie volunteered at an animal shelter, where she had learned a lot about dogs of all ages. "Is it a boy or a girl?"

"He's a boy," said Charles. He wasn't surprised

that Lizzie knew what kind of dog it was. She was always studying that "Dog Breeds of the World" poster in her room.

By now, Lizzie was patting Flash, too. "How do you know his name?"

"His owners told us," Becky said.

Then she and Charles told Lizzie and Steph the whole story about Murray and Dot — as much as they knew of it.

"But who's Murray?" asked Lizzie. "And where did he and his wife go?" Lizzie looked puzzled. "Flash looks so healthy and well groomed, it looks like they took good care of him. So why did they leave him here?"

"That's what we've been trying to figure out," Charles said. "But we haven't gotten anywhere." He explained about the bread man and their trip to the store.

"Meanwhile, this puppy needs a home," said Stephanie. By now, Flash was practically in her lap. She seemed to have a way with dogs.

Becky looked excited. "I know! Do you think Mom and Dad would let us —"

"No way," said Stephanie, shaking her head. "They'll say we're just getting used to living here, and it's too early for a pet, and all that. Just like they do when I ask when I'm getting a horse."

"Well then, we'll just have to convince Mom and Dad that it's time to foster another puppy," Lizzie said to Charles.

"But we have Buddy now," Charles said.

Lizzie was nodding. "I know, but Mom promised we could still foster puppies, remember?" She bent to pet Flash again, and he nuzzled her hand. "Border collies are so smart and fun. We *have* to take him home with us."

Flash wasn't sure exactly what the girl was saying, but he knew it was about him, and he knew it was good. Even though he still missed his own people, he was starting to feel safe with these children. But he was tired of being cooped up! He needed to run.

"Hey, where are you going?" Stephanie said suddenly. Flash jumped up and wiggled through the partly open stall door before anybody could stop him.

"Oh, no!" cried Charles as the white tip of Flash's tail disappeared around the corner.

Becky jumped to her feet. "We have to stop him before the grown-ups see him!" she said.

They all ran out of the stall after Flash — but it was too late. He had already dashed out of the barn and into the yard. The dog raced in circles. He ran over the ground so fast, he looked like a black-and-white blur.

Oh, wonderful! There was nothing better than running! What a great game! Flash usually liked to chase other things, but it was fun to be chased, too. He felt the cold air ruffle his fur. It was good to be outside.

"Wait, Flash! Come here!" Charles called, trying to keep his voice low.

"This way, Flash!" called Lizzie.

All four children ran toward the dog. Flash ran even faster. His feet barely seemed to touch the ground.

Then Becky remembered the way Charles had gotten the dog to follow them. "He'll *never* come if we chase him," she said. "We have to run the *other* way, so he's chasing us."

"*Herding* us, you mean!" said Lizzie, her eyes gleaming. "That's what border collies do on farms! They just know how to keep a bunch of sheep together. Farmers use them to move sheep from one place to another." Lizzie jogged away from Flash and toward the barn, waving the others along with her. Sure enough, Flash stopped in his tracks for a moment, then turned and began to chase them.

They were all laughing so hard that they didn't hear the back door open. "Charles! Lizzie!" called Mom. "What on earth are you all doing?" Mom was standing on the back porch, holding the Bean in her arms.

"Oops," said Charles.

CHAPTER SIX

"Let us handle this!" Stephanie hissed to Becky as they headed toward the house to face the grown-ups. Flash trotted behind them, herding them right up to the doorstep.

"She's right," Lizzie whispered to Charles. "They'll listen to us. We're older."

Charles and Becky looked at each other with raised eyebrows. "What did I tell you?" Charles was saying, without any words. Becky nodded. The big sisters had taken over.

Now Aunt Abigail had joined Mom. "Stephanie, what's going on?" she asked. "Where did that dog come from?" Flash was poking his nose into the kitchen.

Flash was curious. There were good smells in here!

"Can he come in?" Stephanie asked. "This is Flash. Somebody just left him here!"

Charles saw Aunt Abigail's face soften. "You mean, he was abandoned? How awful! I've heard that sometimes people leave dogs near farms when they don't want them anymore."

"Abandoned" meant that a dog's owners left it all alone, so the dog had to take care of itself. That wasn't *exactly* what had happened, but nobody corrected Aunt Abigail. "He must be hungry," she went on.

Charles thought of all the leftovers Flash had eaten, plus the puppy food. "Well . . ." he began. Then Lizzie pinched him. Hard. He closed his mouth.

Aunt Abigail sighed. "All right," she said. "Let him in. But — will he get along with Buddy and the Bean?"

Charles happened to know that Buddy couldn't *wait* to play with Flash. And now that Flash felt more at home, he'd probably enjoy Buddy, too.

"I think Buddy and Flash will be fine together," Lizzie said. "But maybe you should keep holding the Bean for now. We don't know how Flash will behave around little kids."

They brought Flash into the kitchen, closing the doors to keep him from running through the house.

"Well, well, well," said Dad, getting up from the table with a big smile. "Who's this?" He knelt down to say hello to Flash.

Uncle Stephen didn't seem as excited. He looked over his glasses at Flash, frowning. "And who does it belong to?" he asked.

"We don't know," Charles said honestly. "But we think he needs a home."

"What do you think, Dad?" Stephanie asked. "Could we keep him? Please?" She had her arms around Flash's neck. Charles could tell that she had really fallen in love with the black-and-white pup. And Flash seemed to like her, too.

This girl was so nice! Flash thought he could sit here next to her forever — especially in this warm, cozy room. As long as he also got to run and chase and play, that is.

"Out of the question," said Uncle Stephen, turning back to his newspaper. "We're just getting settled here."

Stephanie turned to Aunt Abigail. "Mom?" she asked.

Aunt Abigail was shaking her head. "I don't know, Steph. This dog has a *lot* of energy. I saw him zooming around the backyard, chasing after you all. I'm not sure we can keep him busy enough."

Uncle Stephen was nodding. "A dog like this belongs on a real farm, like over at the Barclays'."

He sighed, turning to Mrs. Peterson. "You've seen that place, right? The one at the other end of the road, where the sheep are always getting loose?"

Charles realized that Stephanie was probably right. Uncle Stephen would never agree to adopting a dog — at least, not this one. He watched Stephanie and Becky petting Flash. They looked so sad! Charles noticed Mom looking, too.

"Stephen," Mom said carefully. "You should give it a chance. I didn't think our family was ready for a dog, either. But we just love Buddy."

Uncle Stephen shook his head stubbornly. "Fine for you," he said. Suddenly Charles realized something funny: His mother was Uncle *Stephen's* bossy older sister!

Charles looked at Mom. "So?" he asked.

"Oh, no!" said Mom.

"Oh, yes," said Charles. "Can't we foster Flash? Just until we find out —"

Lizzie interrupted, "Just until we find the right home?" She gave Charles a glance.

He knew she was warning him not to tell the grown-ups about Murray and Dot. That would just complicate things. Anyway, they wanted to solve the mystery themselves.

"He's a great puppy," Charles finished. "And he'd make a great friend for Buddy."

"Uppy!" shouted the Bean, struggling to get down and pet Flash.

"But . . . we don't even know if Buddy and Flash will get along!" said Mom.

"Let's take them outside and find out!" said Lizzie. She winked at Charles, and Charles winked back. He and Lizzie both knew that Mom was going to agree. They were going to have a new foster puppy.

Sure enough, by the end of the afternoon it was all settled. Not only did Flash and Buddy get along but Flash loved the Bean, too. The border collie would be riding back to Littleton in the van with the Petersons. Not only that, Stephanie and Becky were coming to visit the very next weekend!

CHAPTER SEVEN

Back at home, Charles and Lizzie helped Flash get used to things. Before long, he seemed to feel completely at home. He and Buddy played together for hours in the backyard, and Flash herded the Bean all over the house. The week went by almost before Charles knew it, and soon it was time for Becky and Steph's visit. On Saturday morning, Charles and Lizzie and their dad went to meet their cousins at the Littleton bus station.

"So, where's Flash, and when are we going to the mall?" Stephanie asked, about one second after she and Becky stepped off the bus that had brought them from their country home. "I have all my birthday money with me, plus a gift certificate for the Gap. I cannot *wait* to shop. And I can't wait to see Flash. I brought him a rawhide bone. I bet he misses me."

Whoa! Charles looked over at Becky, and Becky shrugged. Was Stephanie going to be like this all weekend? She was just as bossy as a visitor as she was at her own house. He had been looking forward to seeing his cousins and doing some more detective work, but now he wasn't so sure.

"Flash is at home with Buddy," Charles told Steph. "They're real pals already. They play together all day long."

"That Flash is so smart!" Lizzie boasted. "He's already learned all kinds of tricks. Wait till you see how good he is at shaking hands. I taught him in about five minutes."

"He's smart all right," said Dad as he carried his nieces' backpacks over to the van. "Maybe too smart for his own good. It only took him about an hour to figure out how to get out of our yard through the one tiny hole in the fence."

"Uh-oh," said Stephanie.

"Yes, uh-oh," said Dad. "That dog absolutely *lives* to run and chase things. I'm afraid he'll start chasing cars if he gets the chance." He started up the van and, after making sure everybody was settled in, turned toward home.

"We'll keep him from running off," Charles promised his father. He turned to his cousins. "Flash is great at chasing balls, too. He could do it all day. As long as you keep throwing something, he'll keep running after it. I just wish we had a bigger yard for him to run in."

"That's why I want to take him with us to the stable today," Lizzie said.

"What?" Stephanie looked surprised.

"Oh. I forgot to tell you. I have a riding lesson at noon, so we can't go to the mall today," Lizzie explained. She had already told her cousin all about the lessons she had been taking, and about her wonderful teacher, Kathy. "But it'll be fun! You can meet all the horses, and maybe you can even ride a little. And Kathy said we could bring

Flash to the stable. They have a big indoor riding ring where it will be safe for him to run around."

"We'll go, too," Charles said to Becky. "You can meet Rascal!" He had already told his cousin all about Rascal, a wild little Jack Russell terrier that the Petersons had fostered. They had tried and tried to teach him good indoor manners, but he was just too full of energy and personality. He ended up living at the stable with Kathy and her husband, Wayne. The stable was the perfect place for him. Rascal even had a horse for a best friend!

"My friend Maria and her dad are picking us up in an hour," Lizzie told Stephanie.

"Okay," said Stephanie. "You know I love horses. But I definitely love shopping, too!"

"I'll drive you to the mall tomorrow morning," Dad promised.

"Deal," said Stephanie, sitting back in her seat with a satisfied smile.

* * *

Back at home, the cousins played with Buddy and Flash in the backyard until Maria and her dad arrived. "Can we all fit in your car?" Lizzie asked when they came to the door. "Flash and Buddy, too?"

"Me! Me!" shouted the Bean. He hated to be left behind.

Maria's dad smiled as he counted on his fingers. "Six kids and two dogs?" he asked. "Hmmm . . ."

"Maybe you and Buddy should stay home with me," Mom said to the Bean. His face crumpled and he took a deep breath, getting ready to scream.

"I bet Buddy will let you play with his new ball!" Charles said quickly. Becky and Stephanie had brought a toy for Buddy, too: a fuzzy purple-and-white soccer ball.

The Bean cheered up right away. Mom gave Charles a grateful look. "Have fun!" she said, waving as they piled into the car. It was crowded in the backseat, especially with Flash trying to run from side to side so he could see every single thing they drove past. Now that Flash felt more at home with the Petersons, he was less shy and more excited about seeing new things.

What an interesting world! So much to look at, so much to learn about. Look! Look at those people walking! Maybe they need someone to herd them! Someone to help them find their way!

When they got to the stables, Maria led the way to the indoor riding ring. "I bet that's where we'll find Kathy," she said. Charles had to hold Flash's leash tightly as the strong little dog pulled him this way and that, checking out every little thing.

The ring was inside a big barn. When Maria pulled open the door, Charles saw that it was one wide-open space inside, with white wooden jumps arranged on a soft dirt floor. It was big enough for a dozen horses to ride around in, but at the moment there were no horses in the ring. Just one wild puppy — Rascal.

As soon as they walked in, the little terrier started barking wildly. Rascal was small, but he had a big bark. Charles saw Kathy and Rascal down at the far end of the building. He waved. Rascal kept barking as they walked closer, and Flash kept pulling at the leash.

"Oh, Rascal," Kathy said. "You hush and be nice to our guests." She smiled and said hello. "And this must be Flash," she said. "What a beautiful border collie!"

Flash was pulling harder. He wanted to get closer to the thing Rascal was standing on. So did Charles. He was curious about it, too! It looked like a giant purple seesaw, painted yellow at each end. While Charles watched, Rascal ran up from the bottom end of the wide board. The seesaw tipped when Rascal was in the middle, and he scrambled down the other side, still barking. "Wow!" said Charles. Rascal ran right over to him to say hello, sniff the new dog, and get a pat.

"Cool!" said Stephanie. "I've never seen a dog do anything like that!"

"It's a sport called agility," Kathy explained. "It's like an obstacle course for dogs. This is a teeter-totter, just one of the obstacles. Rascal and I are practicing on our own. Tomorrow my agility group will meet here, and we'll set up the rest of the equipment. There are all kinds of things to climb over and jump through. Dogs love it!" She looked at Flash. "Especially dogs like him. There are a lot of border collies in my group."

"Flash loves to run," Charles said.

"I bet," said Kathy. "Border collies have a lot of energy and are very smart. They can really be a handful unless they have a job. They need something to do. They're great at herding sheep. Farmers breed them to do just that. Have you ever seen the movie *Babe*?"

"The one about the pig that herds sheep?" Stephanie asked.

"Right!" said Kathy. "It has a lot of border collie

action in it. You should watch it again! Anyway, there are things border collies can do if they're not herding sheep. They can stay busy chasing balls or Frisbees. Or they can do agility! They *love* that. Why don't you come watch the agility group tomorrow? You'll meet lots of border collies and their owners."

"I'd love to," said Lizzie, "but we kind of have plans. Maybe some other time?"

"Sure," said Kathy. "For now, why don't you go saddle up your horse? It's time for your lesson."

CHAPTER EIGHT

Charles woke up the next morning thinking about jelly beans. Sour green-apple jelly beans, to be exact. They were his favorite. He loved them. And there was only one place you could get them in Littleton: at the Sweet Dreams candy store, at the mall. For that reason, he didn't mind that Stephanie wanted to go shopping.

"Hey, Buddy," he said, reaching down to pat the puppy that lay on the rug next to his bed. At first, Buddy was too young to make it through the night without going outside, so he had slept in a crate in the kitchen. Mom had gone down to let him out at least once in the middle of the night. But now, Buddy was completely housetrained. He never — well, *hardly* ever — made a mistake. So he was allowed to sleep wherever he wanted to. And he usually wanted to sleep in Charles's room.

Buddy licked Charles's hand sleepily for a moment as Charles petted his silky ears. Then he jumped up and started attacking Charles's fingers.

Oh, boy! Was it morning already? Morning was Buddy's favorite time of day. When Charles woke up, it was playtime! And then came breakfast time! Yay! Buddy loved *morning.*

"Hey!" Charles said. Buddy always woke up so fast! And what was the first thing he wanted to do as soon as he woke up? Play. The second thing? Go outside to pee, then dash back inside for breakfast. "Okay, okay," said Charles, climbing out of his warm, cozy bed. Having a puppy was a lot of responsibility sometimes, but it was worth it.

Lizzie, Stephanie, and Becky were already out in the backyard with Flash when Charles and

Buddy got downstairs. "Watch this!" Lizzie said. She made Flash sit and stay. Then she stepped back and threw a ball to him. He snatched it out of the air and caught it neatly in his mouth. His tail wagged, and he seemed to smile at them.

Charles and the girls cheered.

Flash lay down and let the ball drop out of his mouth, holding it between his paws. He looked down at the ball, then up at Lizzie.

The ball — Lizzie.

The ball — Lizzie.

His gaze was intense.

Throw it again! Throw it again! Now, now, now! Flash couldn't believe how slow people were sometimes. He liked this girl a lot, but didn't she understand that he wanted to catch the ball again? Right now?

Buddy finished peeing and sniffing around the backyard, then loped over to wrestle with his new friend Flash. The two puppies tumbled and ran for a few minutes.

"Have you found out anything else about who Murray is and where he went?" Lizzie asked Steph. It was the first time the cousins had had a chance to talk privately together about the mystery.

"Not a thing," Steph reported.

"I've asked all my friends if they'd ever met a dog named Flash," Becky said, "but nobody knew him."

"So what's next?" Lizzie asked.

"He needs a home. Maybe we should tell Mom and Dad —" Charles began.

"No!" all three girls yelled.

Just then, Buddy seemed to remember that it was breakfast time. He ran to the back door, and Flash followed him.

Inside, Dad was making waffles. "As soon as we finish breakfast, I'll take you to the mall," he said.

"Great!" said Charles as he poured puppy chow into two dishes.

"Sounds like fun!" said Becky. Charles had told her about the jelly beans at Sweet Dreams.

"Well . . ." said Stephanie. "I'm not so sure I want to go, after all." She reached down to pet Flash. "For one thing, Flash can't go to the mall. So really, how much fun could it be?"

Flash heard his name and knew that the girl was talking about him. He looked up at her and nuzzled her hand. Maybe soon she would take him outside and throw the ball some more!

"Fine with me!" Lizzie said. Charles knew his sister did not like going to the mall. What did she care if he got his jelly beans or not? "What do you want to do instead?" Lizzie asked her cousin.

"Go back to the stable and watch those agility

dogs Kathy told us about," Stephanie said right away. "I'm dying to see what they do."

"All right!" said Lizzie. Charles knew Mom had told her to be nice to Stephanie and do whatever her guest wanted. He guessed that Lizzie was happy now that Steph wanted to go to the barn and he was sure Lizzie wanted to do the exact same thing! "I'll call Maria," Lizzie added. "I'm sure she'll want to come."

"So do I!" said Charles. He didn't mind missing out on jelly beans if it meant being around dogs. He knew Buddy would have to stay home again. At least Flash could go with them, since Kathy had invited him.

"Me, too!" said Becky.

"I guess it's our turn to drive five kids and a dog!" Mom said, laughing.

When Dad pulled up near the stable later that morning, the parking area was full. Charles heard dogs barking as soon as he climbed out of the van. "Hear that, Flash?" he asked the puppy at the end of the leash.

Flash sure did. His ears were up and his nose was twitching. He couldn't wait to see what all the fuss was about. He pulled at the leash.

Let's go, let's go! Let's go, go, go!

Charles and Becky followed the older girls into the barn, slipping through the door carefully so no dogs would escape. "Wow!" said Charles when he saw how different the indoor riding area looked.

Big, colorful wooden obstacles filled the space. There was the teeter-totter they'd seen the day before, but now there were also all kinds of jumps, a tunnel for the dogs to run through, and a steep A-frame for them to go up and over. All the equipment was painted bright colors: blue, purple, green, and yellow.

Dogs and people were running around. Dogs climbed over some obstacles and ran through others, while their people yelled encouragement. Some dogs barked happily, while others looked very serious as they charged around.

Charles wondered about a row of white poles standing straight up out of the ground. While he watched, a small, sleek border collie and his owner approached the poles. When the owner pointed at the poles, the dog ran in and out between them, weaving his way from one end of the row to the other. "Did you see that?" Charles asked, turning to Becky. She was nodding. Her eyes were wide.

Kathy walked over, with Rascal at her heels. The little dog's eyes were bright, and his tail was waving. "Welcome!" she said. "I'm so glad you came back. What do you think?"

"I think this looks like the most fun thing in the world," said Stephanie. "If I were a dog, I'd love it!" She couldn't take her eyes off the border collie, who was now dashing through a round tunnel. He came out at the other end and flew over three jumps in a row, sailing through the air as easily as a bird.

"I agree," said Kathy, laughing. "The dogs love it, and so do we. Did you see that border collie do the weave poles?"

They all nodded. So that's what they were called.

"That's one of the harder obstacles for dogs to learn," Kathy said. "But a smarty like Flash would probably pick it up in no time." She bent to pat his head. Flash licked her hand, but his eyes were focused on the activity in the middle of the barn.

"You mean, Flash could be doing this?" Becky asked. "But he's just a puppy!"

"Puppies can't do everything on the agility course right away," Kathy explained. "For example, they shouldn't jump, because their bones are still growing. But lots of these dogs started before they were three months old! Puppies can start by doing something easy, like learning how to run through a tunnel," she went on. "You can use a play tunnel made for little kids. They have them over at the toy store."

Charles knew that they all still wanted to find Flash's mystery owner. But if that didn't work, maybe someone who did agility would adopt him. Charles had a feeling Flash would like that.

Yes! Flash saw a dog jumping through a round thing hung on ropes, then scampering up and over the A-frame. I want to do that!

CHAPTER NINE

On the way home, Charles and Lizzie talked their dad into stopping at the toy store. "A tunnel will be great for Flash," said Charles.

"It will help him burn off energy," Lizzie promised.

"Okay, okay," Dad said.

"And can we pick up a movie to watch later, too?" Lizzie asked.

"Yeah! We want to watch *Babe*!" Stephanie said. "Did you know there are border collies in that movie?"

"Talking pigs, too," Dad said with a grin. "I seem to remember that."

By the time they arrived home with a bright yellow tunnel in the back of the van and a copy of

Babe in Lizzie's backpack, Flash was definitely ready for a good run. Buddy was excited, too. He had been cooped up all morning.

"Playtime!" Charles said. He called Sammy to tell him to bring his dogs over, too. Goldie was a young golden retriever that the Petersons had fostered, and Rufus was an older golden. They both lived next door with Sammy, and they loved to play with other dogs.

With Buddy and Flash still inside, Lizzie and Stephanie set up the tunnel while Charles and Becky made sure the gate to the fence was closed so Flash couldn't get out of the yard. By the time Sammy arrived with Rufus and Goldie, they were all set.

"Let 'em out!" said Charles, opening the back door. Flash and Buddy tumbled down the back stairs and dashed over to greet Rufus and Goldie. Then all four dogs ran around the yard, barking joyfully.

Rufus, the oldest dog, galumphed along slowly,

wagging his feathery tail. Goldie never strayed far from her friend's side, but she had to trot to keep up with the bigger dog. Flash was as quick as lightning. He made three circles around the yard before Rufus and Goldie had even finished one. And Buddy did his best to keep up with all the bigger dogs, without getting run over by any of them. Charles couldn't stop laughing. He could have watched the dogs play together all day.

"What's that?" Sammy asked, pointing to the tunnel.

Charles explained about agility. "It's the coolest!" he said. "Wait till you see Flash zoom through that thing."

"Well, we have to teach him how before he can do it like those dogs at the stable. But let's let him burn off a little more energy first," Lizzie said. She rummaged in her pockets for some tiny biscuits. When the dogs finally slowed down a bit, she gave them each a treat. Then she called them over to the tunnel.

"Now we'll just get them used to it, before we ask them to run through. Look at this!" she said, kneeling down by the tunnel's opening. "What's this?" She put a treat just inside the tunnel. All four dogs dove for it at the same time, knocking Lizzie over.

Stephanie and the others cracked up.

"Hmm," said Lizzie. "Maybe we should try one dog at a time."

"Flash gets to go first!" insisted Stephanie.

Sammy put Rufus and Goldie on their leashes and let Becky hold Goldie's. Charles picked up Buddy, cradling the soft little puppy in his arms. "You have to wait your turn," he said into Buddy's ear.

Charles watched as Lizzie tried again, putting another treat just inside the tunnel for Flash. *Zip!* Flash stuck his head into the tunnel and the treat was gone. Flash didn't seem scared of the tunnel at all.

"Steph, come hold him at one end!" said Lizzie.

"I'll go to the other end and call him. We'll see if he'll run all the way through the tunnel to come to me."

Stephanie knelt down by the opening of the tunnel, her hand on Flash's collar. Lizzie went to the other end. "Here, Flash!" she called.

Flash heard his name. He looked around to see who was calling. It was Lizzie! She always had the best treats! When Stephanie let go of his collar, Flash raced as fast as he could toward Lizzie. But — why was she laughing so hard? What about his treat?

"Flash! You were supposed to go *through* the tunnel, not around it!" Lizzie said. She gave him the treat, anyway.

"I'll show him!" said Sammy, handing Rufus's leash to Charles. "Follow me, Flash!" Flash ran around to see what Sammy was doing. Before anyone could stop him, Sammy crawled through the tunnel on his hands and knees.

Flash could see that the boy needed herding. If that meant he had to go through the tunnel after him, so what? It looked like fun.

Flash scrambled through the tunnel right after Sammy.

"Yes! Good dog!" Lizzie cried. She gave Flash three treats. She didn't give Sammy any, even though he pretended to beg like a dog.

Buddy struggled to get down. He loved being held by Charles, but right now he just had to go find out more about that thing Flash was running through.

"Whoa! Okay, little guy," Charles said, putting Buddy down on the ground. "Here comes Buddy!" he called.

Becky let Rufus and Goldie go, too. All the dogs charged for the tunnel. Now that they knew what they were supposed to do, they couldn't wait to run through it over and over again, especially since Lizzie was at the other end, handing out treats. Soon the dogs were zooming through the tunnel, one right after the other and sometimes two or three at a time. Flash almost always brought up the rear, barking happily at the heels of the other three dogs.

"He's herding them, see?" Lizzie pointed out. "Flash is a real border collie." She sounded proud.

What a scene! Soon everybody joined Lizzie at the end of the tunnel to watch the dogs come through. Charles laughed as he watched Buddy's funny face poke out of the tunnel. The puppy looked so happy.

Goldie's head popped out next.

Then Rufus trotted out of the tunnel, shaking his big old head.

"Hey, where's Flash?" Stephanie asked.

Everybody looked around. Where *was* that quick little black-and-white dog?

He wasn't in the tunnel. He wasn't behind the lilac bush. He wasn't on the porch.

Flash was not in the yard.

CHAPTER TEN

"He must have gotten out again!" Charles said. But how? Dad had fixed the hole in the fence. Then Charles noticed that the gate near the side of the house was hanging open. "Look! That gate was definitely shut," he said. "Flash must have figured out how to push it open."

"Oh, no!" said Becky.

"We'd better find him, quick!" said Stephanie.

"You and Sammy and Becky go toward Elm Street," Lizzie said to Charles. "We'll go toward Maple."

Charles didn't even pause to glare at Lizzie for being bossy. She was right. They had to find Flash right away. He could get hurt out on the street. He ran for the gate. "Flash!" Charles yelled.

Becky was the fastest runner. She dashed through the gate, and disappeared around the corner of the house. The others followed after her. As Charles rounded the corner, he saw Becky and a woman leaning over Flash, who was lying on the sidewalk.

Charles groaned. All of a sudden, he felt dizzy and faint. Flash was hurt! It was partly his fault for not watching him more closely. But it was hard to keep track of a dog like Flash. He was so quick and so smart. He could escape from anywhere.

"He's okay, he's okay," Becky called. "He was just saying hello." Sure enough, there weren't any cars close by. They were lucky this time. When Charles got close enough, he could see that Flash was lying on his back, grinning up at Becky and the woman.

"Sweet dog," said the woman, giving Flash's belly one more pat as she stood up again. "I was just walking by. He ran right up to me and rolled over for a tummy rub."

Charles let out a big sigh of relief. "Well, I guess he's not quite as shy as he used to be!" He tried to smile.

"Flash really needs a home where he'll be safe," Mom said, later that night, when they were all sitting down to a dinner of lasagna and salad. "If we can't find one very soon, I think we'll have to take him over to Caring Paws."

That was the animal shelter where Lizzie volunteered. It was not a bad place, but Charles hated to think of Flash locked up all day in one of the big cages there.

"We'll find something," Becky promised. She looked over at Charles. He knew what she was thinking. They *had* to solve the mystery of where Flash belonged. The sooner, the better!

After dinner, the four cousins settled into the living room to watch their movie. A tired-out Flash lay with his head on Stephanie's knee, and Buddy cuddled in Charles's lap. Lizzie put *Babe* on, and before long everyone was swept up into the story of the little pig who was brought up by a loving border collie.

"Look, Flash, that dog looks just like you!" said Stephanie. She gave him a kiss on the head, and Flash thumped his tail.

When the movie was over, the cousins went into the kitchen for ice cream. "I wish Flash could live on a farm," Charles said as he got the chocolate sauce out of the fridge. "He would *love* to herd sheep, like that dog in the movie."

"Those silly sheep remind me of the Barclays' sheep, the ones that are always getting out. They sure could use some herding." Steph was scooping vanilla fudge into her bowl.

"The Barclays? Where do they live?" Lizzie asked.

"Right up the road," Becky said as she reached for the chocolate sauce. "You know, the house that looks just like ours? People are always getting lost and knocking on our door by mistake, when they really want to be at the Barclays."

Charles stared at Becky. "Wait, what did you just say?" He put down his spoon.

Becky laughed. "That the Barclays' house looks like ours?" she asked. "So?" Then, suddenly, her eyes lit up. "Oh!" she said. She put a hand over her mouth. "That's it!" she cried. "Murray and his wife must have meant to leave Flash at the Barclays' farm instead of ours!"

The mystery was solved. And the next day, instead of a trip to the mall, the Petersons and their cousins headed back to the country, taking Flash to the home he was meant for. Instead of turning right where the road forked to Uncle Stephen's place, Dad drove up the left-hand fork to the farm at the other end of the road. This one had an old farmhouse and an old barn just like

Stephanie and Becky's, but there was a cow in the pasture and geese in the yard, and Dad had to swerve almost all the way off the road when a flock of sheep came trotting up to meet the van.

When they pulled up at the farm, Charles opened the van door and Flash jumped out as if he knew he was home. He dashed toward the sheep and started chasing them back to their pen.

"Go get 'em!" yelled Mr. Barclay, laughing out loud as he watched the sleek dog run.

Mr. Barclay turned out to be a tall, smiling man who looked a lot like the farmer in *Babe*. He and his wife were thrilled to meet Flash! He said that Murray and Dot had called them on Friday to make sure Flash was happy living there. Ever since, they'd been frantically trying to figure out where the dog had gone.

"I can't believe it," Mr. Barclay was saying for the fourth time, as he looked down at Flash. "I've been calling around everywhere, looking for a lost dog. I never *imagined* that Dot and Murray might have left him off at your place instead of mine. When we called your place, no one answered."

Dad was shaking his head. Charles hoped he wasn't going to start lecturing again about how the cousins should not have kept secrets from their parents. Uncle Stephen and Aunt Abigail had been out of town for the weekend, so they weren't there to talk to the Barclays. But everything had worked out fine in the end, hadn't it?

Becky gave Charles a high five. "We solved the mystery!" she said.

"We're sure glad you did! Flash is a beauty," said Mrs. Barclay. "We've always had border collies, but our last one died six months ago. We really need a dog to help with our sheep. That's why we told Murray that we'd be happy to adopt Flash when he moved. Little did we know that Murray and Dot would have to leave so suddenly."

Stephanie knelt down to hug Flash. Charles thought she looked really sad.

"Of course, you're welcome to come visit with him anytime," said Mr. Barclay. He must have noticed Stephanie's face, too. "I'll be training him to herd the sheep, but he'll want to play, too."

Stephanie smiled, looking happier already. "I — I'd like to try to teach him how to do agility," she said. "Have you ever heard of that?"

"Heard of it!" said Mrs. Barclay. "I *love* it. Our last dog was a champion. Want to help me train Flash? I still have lots of the equipment put away in our barn."

"Really?" Stephanie asked. Her face lit up. Charles had a feeling that she was going to be a lot happier living in the country from now on. So what if there weren't any stores? If she had a dog to play with — even if it wasn't hers — Stephanie wouldn't miss the mall. And maybe someday soon she and Becky would get a dog of their own, once Uncle Stephen saw how responsible they both could be.

Not only was the mystery solved, but Flash had a wonderful home where he could run and play safely. Plus, he had a job! Just what he needed. Stephanie and Becky could see him every day, and Charles and Lizzie would see him whenever they visited their cousins. The Petersons had helped another puppy find the perfect place.

PUPPY TIPS

There are so many fun things you can do with your puppy, no matter what kind of dog you own! Border collies like Flash love to do agility or play flyball. Dogs with great noses, like bloodhounds or German shepherds, love to do tracking. Golden retrievers enjoy obedience training. Dogs that love to run are good at lure coursing, where they chase after a pretend rabbit. Some dogs even love to dance with their owners! Dancing with dogs is known as freestyle.

You can find out more about all of these activities at the library or on the internet. Or, you can just take your puppy for a good long walk. *Every* dog loves that!

Dear Reader,

My dog, Django, has a friend named Bodi who is a border collie. She looks just like Flash: black and white and sleek. Bodi is very smart and very fast! I thought Django was a fast runner until I saw Bodi chase a ball.

Bodi likes to be busy all the time, so it is a good thing that her owner can take her to work every day. She makes sure that everybody who comes to the office gets a big greeting!

Yours from the Puppy Place,
Ellen Miles

ABOUT THE AUTHOR

Ellen Miles lives in Vermont. She is the author of *The Pied Piper* and other Scholastic Classics, and she is also writing another series for Scholastic titled Taylor-Made Tales.

Ellen has always loved a good story. She also loves biking, skiing, and playing with her own dog, Django. Django is a black Lab who would rather eat a book than read one.

DON'T MISS THE NEXT PUPPY PLACE ADVENTURE!

Meet Scout, an adorable German shepherd puppy with a talent for helping people.

"Let's play hide-and-seek with Scout and Buddy!" Charles said. "That's a good way to train Scout to be a Search and Rescue dog. I'll go hide behind that tree, and you send Scout and Buddy to find me."

When Charles was hidden, Lizzie called the puppies. Scout came running, but Buddy was still busy sniffing around. "Oh, well," said Lizzie. "Scout's the one we really want to train. Go find Charles, Scout! Find him!"

Scout looked up at the girl. She wanted something. What was it?

"Here, I'll show you," said Lizzie. "Let's find him together!" She ran, leading Scout closer to where Charles was hiding. "Find him!" she said again, hoping to teach Scout what that meant.

Scout sniffed. She smelled the very special, wonderful scent of someone she loved. Charles! She bounced around the tree. There he was! She jumped up happily, barking. How wonderful to find her boy! And now he was giving her some treats. Yum!

"I think she gets the idea," said Lizzie. "She sure is a fast learner. Let's try again. I'll distract her while you hide." Lizzie looked around for Buddy and spotted him over by some big boulders. He looked happy enough, exploring on his own. He didn't seem interested in hide-and-seek, but that was okay.

Charles ran off again and hid himself behind a

bush. After a minute, Lizzie told Scout to "Find him!" Scout took off like a rocket — straight for the bush.

Hide and seek with Scout was so much fun. Charles hid again, and then Lizzie hid twice. Scout got better and better at finding them quickly. It was hard to fool her! She could sniff them out no matter how well they hid. Her nose was amazing.

Finally, when both Charles and Lizzie had run out of puppy treats, they plopped down on the ground for a rest. Scout put her head on Charles's knee and stretched out one paw onto Lizzie's leg. Lizzie scratched the puppy's ears. "Great job, Scout," she said. "Maybe you can teach Buddy how to do it, too."

"Where is Buddy?" Charles asked. "Buddy!" he called.

Lizzie expected Buddy to come galloping over. But he didn't. She started calling, too. "Buddy! Where are you?"

"Maybe he thinks he's playing hide-and-seek," said Charles.

Lizzie called again. She knew Buddy had to be somewhere nearby. After all, the whole area was fenced in. But suddenly, she was beginning to worry. How could she have let him wander off? She felt terrible. She had gotten so wrapped up in training Scout that she had forgotten — just for a moment — about the most important little puppy in the world: her puppy, Buddy!